Curious George®
Subway Train Adventure

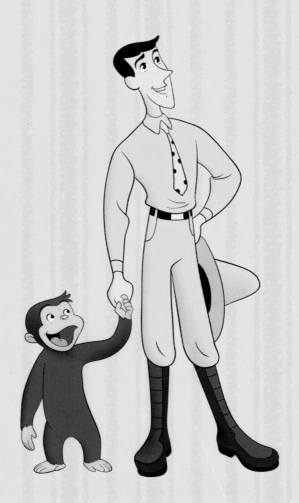

Adaptation by Julie M. Fenner
Based on the TV series teleplay written by Lazar Saric

Houghton Mifflin Harcourt
Boston   New York

ISBN: 978-0-544-78585-4 paper-over-board
ISBN: 978-0-544-80032-8 paperback

Design by Lauren Pettapiece

www.hmhco.com
Manufactured in China
SCP 10 9 8 7 6 5 4 3 2 1
4500603271

AGES	GRADES	GUIDED READING LEVEL	READING RECOVERY LEVEL	LEXILE ® LEVEL
5-7	1	J	17	430L

George was up early.
Today they were going to the zoo.

"We are taking the subway," said the
man with the yellow hat.
It was George's first subway ride.

"The subway is a train that runs under the ground," said the man. "It takes people—and little monkeys—to places all over the city."

George could not wait to see the trains.
He ran down the stairs, through the
gate, and right into a police officer!

"Wait, George! We have to pay first,"
the man called.
"It's okay. Monkeys ride for free," said
the officer.

They walked to the track and waited.
George was confused.
Where was the train?

"Don't worry, George," said the man. "The train should be here soon. Let's go look at the map."

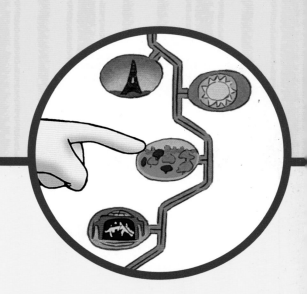

"We are here at Endless Park Station. We are going to take the train all the way up to the zoo."

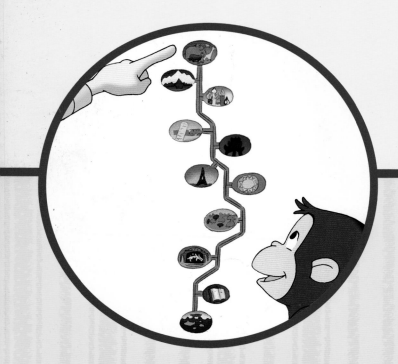

"Would you like a subway map of your own?" asked the man. George nodded his head yes. "Okay. Wait here."

While George waited, a train pulled into the station. George was so excited to get on the train, that he forgot to wait for his friend.

The man saw George on the train, but
the doors closed before he could get on.
"I'll meet you at the next station,"
shouted the man.

George wasn't worried.
He decided to explore the train.
"Hello there," said the conductor.
"Would you like to help me drive
the train?"

"This is how I control the speed, brakes, and doors," she explained. George honked the horn and moved the lever forward. The train started.

George got off at the next station. The
man's train arrived, but there were too
many people for him to exit. "I'll wait for
you at the next stop," the man called.

Honk! Honk! George was curious. He could hear the next train coming, but where was it? He turned around and saw one behind him. He climbed aboard.

At the next stop,
George realized he
was back at Endless Park.
How did he get there?

Luckily, the police officer was there to help. "The track with the up arrow goes uptown to the zoo. The track with the down arrow goes downtown to Fisherman's Wharf." Now George knew to follow the up arrow!

When his train stopped in a tunnel, George saw his friend on another train. "George! Take the train all the way to the zoo!" shouted the man.

Finally he arrived at the zoo stop.
The man was there too.

George loved riding the subway, but next time he would stay close to his friend.

Imagination Station

Using a blank sheet of paper and crayons, make up an imaginary subway map for a train to follow. Decide how many stations it will have and what their names are. What would riders see at each station on your map?

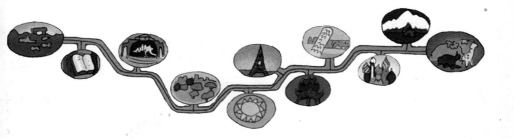

Did you know?

● The first U.S. subway opened in Boston, Massachusetts, on September 1, 1897.

● If you put the New York City transit tracks end to end, they would stretch from New York City to Chicago, Illinois.

● The high-speed "bullet trains" in Japan can go over 300 miles per hour.

● There is a train that travels through the Channel Tunnel, 250 feet underwater, between England and France.

Make a Name Train!

You can make your own name train with a few basic supplies! Ask a parent or another grownup for help.

You will need . . .
a blank piece of paper
construction paper in different colors
a pen or pencil
scissors
crayons or markers
glue

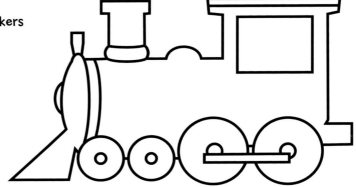

What to do:
1. Use a pen or pencil to trace the train engine above onto the left end of your blank paper or draw an engine of your own. Use your crayons or markers to color it in.
2. Cut out different colored squares of construction paper for each letter of your name and then use crayons or markers to write the letters out on your squares.
4. Cut out small black circles for your train's wheels.
5. Glue the letters of your name down in the right order behind your engine.
6. Glue two wheels down on each letter square. Now your name train is ready to ride. *Choo-Choo!*

24